DATE DUE

THE
NUTCRACKER

Retold by
Pat Whitehead
Illustrated by
Beverly Rich

Troll Associates

Library of Congress Cataloging in Publication Data

Whitehead, Patricia.
    The nutcracker.

    Based on Peter Ilich Tchaikovsky's Shchelkunchik.
    Summary: When a young girl rescues her nutcracker
from an attack by mice, the nutcracker becomes a
prince and takes her to the fabulous Kingdom of
Sweets.
    [1. Fairy tales]   I. Rich, Beverly, ill.
II. Tchaikovsky, Peter, Ilich, 1840-1893.
Shchelkunchik.   III. Title.
PZ8.W5799Nu   1988   [E]   87-10916
ISBN 0-8167-1063-5 (lib. bdg.)
ISBN 0-8167-1064-3 (pbk.)

Copyright © by Troll Associates

10   9   8   7   6   5   4   3   2

THE
NUTCRACKER

A long time ago, in a land not so very far away, lived a little girl named Marie. Marie loved to play games and dance and draw pretty pictures. But, most of all—more than anything else—Marie loved Christmas.

One year, on Christmas Eve, Marie's father and mother had a party. Everyone in the village was there. There was music and dancing and all sorts of games and magic tricks. A huge tree filled the room and glittered with sparkling lights and tinsel.

Beneath the tree, in all shapes and colors, were the presents. When the time came to open them, the children quickly tore away the bright paper. What treasures they found! There were shiny brass trumpets and big fuzzy bears; lovely china dolls and bright tin soldiers. It was truly a wonderful Christmas.

And yet, the most wonderful part was still to come. Marie had a godfather. His name was Herr Drosselmeyer. Herr Drosselmeyer was a very unusual man. He wore a black patch over his right eye, and his long white hair stuck out wildly from his head. And Herr Drosselmeyer also had a very special skill—he was an excellent toymaker! This Christmas, Herr Drosselmeyer was bringing a special present just for Marie.

All the other gifts had already been opened. The guests were eating cakes and candies. The children were playing with their new toys.

When Herr Drosselmeyer suddenly appeared, the children were afraid—all except Marie. Happily, she ran to give him a hug. And then, he presented her with the best present of all.

"What did you get?"

The children crowded around as Marie quickly opened the small box.

"Ooooh," sighed Marie. "What a lovely little man."

The little man was a Nutcracker. He was dressed as a soldier. His mouth opened and closed. And his teeth were strong enough to crack the hardest of nuts.

"He looks so real," cried the children. It was true. The Nutcracker *did* look real. And yet, he was only made of wood.

Then something awful happened. Fritz, Marie's brother, grabbed the Nutcracker and ran off. Marie took off after him. In the excitement, Fritz dropped the little man.

"Oh, no," cried Marie. "He's broken."

Sure enough, the little Nutcracker's jaw had snapped. Marie was heartbroken.

"Come now, my child," said Herr Drosselmeyer. "He'll be all right. See, I'll just wrap my handkerchief around his head to keep his mouth shut. Don't worry. He'll be as good as new in the morning."

With that, the old man scooped up the broken toy.
He placed it in a tiny bed—just the right size for a Nut-
cracker. Marie sniffled a bit more, but she felt better.
Somehow, she knew Herr Drosselmeyer was right.

As the hour grew late, the guests said good night. And one by one, they left. Marie went upstairs to bed. So did her parents and her brother Fritz. The house became quite still.

But Marie couldn't sleep. Silently, she tiptoed down the stairs to take another peek at her Nutcracker. Marie began to feel a bit uneasy. It was dark downstairs, and very quiet and still. The tree looked so big. And the toys looked so real....

Just then the clock struck midnight. Quickly, Marie turned around. And there, perched on top of the clock, was an owl. And somehow, the owl looked very much like Herr Drosselmeyer.

Marie didn't have much time to wonder about this. All sorts of strange things were happening at once. The Christmas tree grew taller and taller. The room grew larger. And the toys, scattered about the tree, began to move. The soldiers and the dolls—and even the Nutcracker—were all coming to life!

Marie could hardly believe her eyes. But that wasn't all. She heard strange squeaks and creaks and rustling noises. Suddenly, an army of giant gray mice appeared. Now Marie was really frightened.

The Nutcracker quickly sprang into action. He grabbed a toy sword and led his army of tin soldiers against the mice. It was a fierce battle. The tin soldiers fought bravely. And so did the mice.

Screeeech! Marie heard a sharp whistle. The battle stopped. Everyone turned to see what the noise was. And there, at the foot of the tree, was the most curious creature Marie had ever seen.

It was a giant mouse—much bigger than any of the others. And, instead of one head, it had seven...each wearing a tiny golden crown. This was the Mouse King.

The Mouse King challenged the Nutcracker to a duel.
What a horrible sight! The Nutcracker fought as best he
could. But the ugly beast seemed to be everywhere at
once. Finally, the Nutcracker fell to the ground. And the
Mouse King was just about to pounce on him.

Terrified, Marie threw her slipper at the Mouse King.
He was furious, and now he came after Marie. The poor
girl was so frightened, she fainted. In that same instant,
the Nutcracker bravely killed the Mouse King with his
sword. The battle was over.

Proudly, the Nutcracker held one of the Mouse King's golden crowns above his head. As he did this, the little wooden man changed into a handsome young Prince. At once, everything else began to change, too.

The mice and the toys disappeared. Snow began to fall in great swirling gusts. And, before she knew what was happening, Marie was sailing through space with the Prince.

"Don't be frightened," he told her. "You saved my life. And now I am taking you to see the Kingdom of Sweets."

And so Marie began the most wonderful adventure of all. She and the Prince landed in a beautiful forest. Its trees were filled with thousands of tiny white candles. Lovely ripe fruit hung from all the branches.

"This is the Christmas Forest," said the Prince.

Next, they sailed together in a walnut shell down the River of Lemonade. All along the shore were houses made of candy. The roofs were covered with sugar icing, and the chimneys were made of jelly beans.

"This is all part of the magic land ruled by the Sugar Plum Fairy," explained the Prince.

As he spoke, they came to a magnificent palace. It was made completely of spun sugar. Just then, the Sugar Plum Fairy appeared. She was delighted to see them.

"Come inside," she said. After she had heard the story of their battle with the Mouse King, she said, "We shall celebrate your victory."

Inside the palace, tables were filled with every kind of sweet. There were chocolates and nougats and bonbons of all sizes and flavors. And then, the Sugar Plum Fairy danced for them. What a wonderful dance it was. Marie and the Prince joined in. And, finally, all the sweets and bonbons got up and danced with them.

Marie wished she could stay forever. But soon it was
time to leave. A lovely white sleigh appeared. It was
pulled by magic reindeer. As Marie and the Prince
climbed in, the reindeer flew into the sky. Marie waved
good-bye to the dancing Kingdom of Sweets. And away
she sailed into the snowy night.

Marie climbed higher and higher into the sky. The snow grew thicker and thicker. Everything was white, and Marie felt so sleepy....

On Christmas morning, Marie awoke. There she was in her very own bed. Christmas—the day she loved more than any other—had finally come. Quickly, Marie raced downstairs to see the tree.

And there, in his own little bed, lay the Nutcracker. He was just as she had left him—only he wasn't broken anymore. He was as good as new—just as Herr Drosselmeyer had promised. What a wonderful Christmas surprise!